I0593946

SHORT SHOCKERS

20 Short Stories

by Jacky Dahlhaus

Folla Fiction Publishing

First published online: December 2017
First published in print: September 2018

eBook ISBN: 978-1-9735872-4-8
Print ISBN: 978-0-9956719-9-7

Book Cover Photo by Johannes Plenio of Unsplash
Book Cover Design by Jacky Dahlhaus

jackydahlhaus.com

Books written by Jacky Dahlhaus:

Releasing A Vampire

Living Like A Vampire

Raising A Vampire

Killing A Vampire

Short Shockers

jackydahlhaus.com

Contents

Introduction

The short stories contained in this bundle were written by me as 'homework' for the Meldrum Writers' Club. I joined the club in November 2015, when I took a book on English grammar to the desk of the library and the library lady pointed out to me that there was a writers' club meeting on a regular basis in the library. I had only begun writing recently and thought it sounded interesting. I met the following Monday with 'the group.' It consisted of only one person, Sandy, a pensioner with an interest in writing. He told me it had been a busier group before, but people had moved, gotten sick, or lost interest. It clicked between Sandy and me, and ever since, we have been meeting on a regular basis. The meetings moved from Mondays to Wednesdays and from monthly to almost weekly and the group has grown a little.

Each meeting, we pick a few keywords with which we need to write a thousand words short story. It is a good exercise to consolidate your writing. The story needs a beginning, a middle, and an end, even though it's such a short one. This means no flowery talk with lots of adverbs or adjectives. Sometimes this is really hard as you have an idea in your head you want to convey. The random words really do stimulate your creativity and push you in directions you never thought you'd go. It is also amazing how people can come up with such different stories using the same words.

We are rather lenient with the assignments. Some stories are very short and some a bit longer than the prescribed one-thousand words. We used the word 'duck' twice and the first time I used it in my story, I used it twice: as the bird and the action. The second time we chose the word, I used the French version. It's fun playing with words!

Quite often, we break up the routine and go another route. 'Sinking Ships,' for example, was a story written as a first chapter of a longer story (which still doesn't exist, I'm afraid). 'Reunion' was written with a writing prompt, and 'Three men on a bench' was written as 'a story about three different characters.'

Writing short stories is a lot of fun, and I think it helped me write better over time. Some stories I am proud of, others not so much. Most stories have a 'shocking' twist at the end. They are put in no particular order. I hope you like them. I'd love to hear which one you like best.

Enjoy!

Jacky Dahlhaus

Sinking Ships

<u>Writing Assignment</u>: Write the first chapter of a story
<u>Keywords</u>: ship, satellite, high/hi

My life is like a sinking ship. There is a big hole in it and all who cared for it have jumped overboard to save their own lives. Now the liquid is pouring in and all there is to do is wait.

The door opened, and Sally walked into my office. She put a telephone transcript on my desk. I knew it was a telephone transcript as she always wrote those on yellow paper. In a continuous motion, she took the bottle of Southern Comfort out of my hand, screwed the lid back on, and dropped the bottle in the bottom drawer of my desk.

"We've got a case. Give the woman a call," she said and left.

As she pulled the door shut behind her, the image of her curving hips lingered on my retinas. Sally was my secretary, hovering around me like a satellite around the earth. She was the connection between me and the rest of the world. I was lost without her. Although how long she'd stay, I had no idea. We hadn't had a case for over a month and I hadn't figured out how to pay her yet. There was only so much a girl could take. I figured that one out the hard way.

I picked up the yellow paper and read Sally's writing. The message was short. A name, Lexie Dexter, and a phone number. What would the woman want from me? Find out if her husband had an affair? Find her long-lost relative? All depressing outcomes, no matter how much you prepared them for it. People should leave the past behind them. Nothing good comes from digging it up.

I dialed the number and heard the phone ring on the other end of the line. After the second ring, it was answered.

"Yes," was the only thing she said.

The voice was low, without emotion. A shiver ran down my spine.

"It's Matto, private investigator. You called."

There was a silence for a moment. Was she thinking of backing out? Did she all of a sudden figure it wasn't worth the hassle anymore? Didn't she like the tone of my voice? Women could be so fickle sometimes.

"We need to talk," she said.

"I thought we were."

"I need to show you something," her voice now irritated.

"You know where my office is," I said. It wasn't a question. If she got the phone number, she very likely found it next to the address.

"No, not there. I can't be seen going into your office. Meet me at the Crazy Horse bar. Half an hour." The line went dead.

I stared at the phone. It had been a strange conversation. Normally, the women who were asking for my help would follow my instructions, not the other way around. Why couldn't she be seen coming here? Was it below her ranking? Was it too dangerous? It was not my habit to get involved in any mafia business, but the woman had peaked my interest and wild horses couldn't keep me away from this one, mafia or not. Grabbing my coat, I told Sally I was going out.

"When will you be back?" she asked.

"When I'm thirsty," I replied as I went down the stairs.

The Crazy Horse was an Italian bar. Mafia territory. Why did the broad pick this bar? It was an ill omen. My eyes had to adjust to the darkness inside. One man behind the bar, three at a table at the door, and a few couples scattered around the place. Apart from the entrance, there was one escape exit at the back of the joint.

I ordered an Alabama Slamma and took a seat with my back to the wall. I didn't like surprises. It wasn't long before my new client showed up. When she entered, I knew at once it was her. She was tall, even without the high heels, and had a figure to die for. Marilyn Monroe curves. A faux-fur was slung over her shoulders. In her hands, she clasped a precious stone studded purse. Why the hell did she pick this louche bar when dressing like this? So much for keeping a low profile. She went straight to my table and sat down. One of the customers must have talked. The woman had connections. And money.

She stuck her hand out and said, "Hi, I'm Lexie Dexter."

I shook her hand and noted the scent of her hand cream. It was stronger than the perfume she was wearing. Her nails were well manicured and there were several rings studded with diamonds on her fingers. 'Loaded is more like it,' I thought about the financial status of the woman and the positive prospects of mine.

"Mike Matto," I said. "You wanted to show me something."

The woman looked around her. She took a gun out of her purse and put it on the table. I stared at it. This was not exactly what I had expected. When I looked around, nobody seemed phased by the fact there was a weapon on the table.

"This is the gun that killed my husband an hour ago," she said.

"You should go to the police, lady," I said. I downed my Alabama Slamma and made a move to get out of my seat.

The woman put her hand on my arm.

The skin of her hand was tanned which didn't match the paleness of her face. The tan nor the blush the woman had applied couldn't hide it. She didn't say anything. It was the pleading in her eyes which made me sit back down. They were so much like my Melody's eyes. There was a contradiction to the woman I couldn't pinpoint. She seemed strong, but I wondered if it was all a façade. I figured it couldn't hurt to hear her out and sat down again.

"There was gunpowder on my hands," she continued. "My fingerprints are all over the gun, but I didn't pull the trigger."

Cream Pie

Keywords: salesman, pink, bedroom, cream pie

Samuel was a happy young man. His father owned a bedding store and Sam had recently joined his father's sales department. Theo, his father, had trained him in every department of the store over the past few years. Now Sam was working full-time and he was already seen as a competent salesman by all staff.

He was about to ring the doorbell on his first maintenance visit. He had gotten the call when all the other staff members were busy. The lady on the phone had called to confirm the appointment for 12 noon today. As the others were busy with clients, he had decided to take this task upon himself. He knew his father went on maintenance visits now and again, so he knew it was normal to visit customers. Still, he felt anxious. He didn't really know what was expected on a maintenance visit as this was one topic his father had never divulged anything about it. After he rang the doorbell, a lady opened the door. She was a beautiful woman, scarcely dressed in a pink negligee and a pink, see-through gown. She was clearly taken aback when she saw young Sam.

"Can I help you?" she finally said, slightly embarrassed as she tried to cover her exposed body with the gown.

"Yes, Ms. Smith, my name is Sam, I am here for the mattress maintenance," Sam said, trying to keep his eyes on the woman's face.

"Ah, in that case, you better come in," the woman said, pleased all of a sudden, and she stepped out of the way to let Sam in. She told him to follow her upstairs. Sam did as he was told. Entering the woman's bedroom was as if he entered a fairy tale; everything in the room was pink. Literally. Everything. The curtains were pink, the carpet was pink, the wallpaper was pink, and the bedding was pink. Even all the little, fluffy accessories were pink. On the bedside table was a dish with a cream pie, the only thing in the room that wasn't pink.

"What do I do now?" Sam said unsurely.

"Oh, let me take care of that," she woman said knowledgeable, and she pushed Sam onto the bed. After she had straddled him she started to undress him. "We need to test the bed for squeaks," she smiled. "It's vital for my business."

Sam suddenly realized that this woman was a hooker. He had never been with a woman and couldn't believe his luck that this gorgeous specimen was practically throwing herself at him. What better way to learn than from a professional?

"It would be a pleasure to help you with that," he said delighted, while his pants were being removed, "but... um, is there any cost involved?" He had to know before she moved on as he didn't have any cash on him.

"Nope, all has been paid for in advance," she said assured.

Just as she had her hands on his underwear the doorbell rang. They both looked at the bedroom door.

"Wait here," she said.

Sam thought that was funny. Where else was he going to go in his underpants? Ms. Smith, he still didn't know her first name, left the room and he could hear her letting somebody in. To Sam's despair, he heard them coming up the stairs. He quickly grabbed all his clothing and shoes, looked around, and hid in the wardrobe with the pink painted louver shutters. He could hear the visitor now and realized it was a man. He recognized the man's voice; it was the voice of his father! He had to make sure that what he heard was true, so he peeked through the louvers. To his astonishment, it was indeed his father.

"I'm so glad you came for the maintenance check again, Theo," the woman said.

"Wouldn't want to miss it. It means the world to me, um, the company, of course!" His father and Ms. Smith laughed.

Sam had no choice but to stay put where he was. He saw his father being undressed by the woman, who didn't seem to be surprised that Sam had vanished. After the undressing, there was a lot of giggling and groaning. The giggling happened mostly when Sam's father was using the cream pie to cover the woman's naked body and then taking it all off again, with his tongue. The groaning happened after. He couldn't believe this man was his father. The man who was married to his mother. The man who had lived with his mother for over twenty years and whom he had never seen naked together. The thought of them having sex had never, ever, entered his mind. His mother was the type of woman that nobody would ever think of having sex. She was chubby, didn't use any make-up, and was usually dressed in floral gowns, granny style. After almost being relieved of his virginity by this diva, Sam could understand why his father came here to do his 'maintenance checks.'

Sam made sure his father had left before finally coming out of the wardrobe. Ms. Smith was still lying on the bed, smoking a cigarette.

"I better go now," he said shyly and started to get dressed.

"You don't have to," the woman said with a wicked smile. But Sam left nevertheless. The recent experience had spoilt the moment for him.

That evening during dinner, Sam was very quiet. His mother had cooked a simple stew today. To compensate for her blend cooking, she was proud to put a cream pie on the table for dessert. Sam couldn't contain himself any longer.

"That pie looks delicious, Mom! I'd love to smear it on a woman's body and lick it off!"

His father nearly choked.

"Don't say such vulgarities, Sam, you'll give your father a heart-attack!"

Sam exchanged knowing glances with his father and knew that from that moment on, they would share the load of maintenance visits.

The Apparition

Keywords: daughter/son, supernatural occurrence, pursuit, empty house, shield

My son stood on the lawn in front of our house. His fringe blocked one eye as it always did, and he was wearing his favorite dark-green, grungy T-shirt on top of his tight-fitting jeans. It was mid-November, and it was weird. Not so much that he wasn't wearing a jacket, even though the temperature outside warranted wearing at least some sort of outdoor attire, but more so because he had died last year.

I pulled my phone out of my back pocket and called my husband while keeping the sheers out of my view. I didn't want to let go of the vision.

"Hi honey, what's up?" my husband asked cheerfully. He had recovered sooner from the loss.

"Um, please don't get upset, darling, but Sean is standing on our lawn."

There was a long pause before Bill answered.

"What do you mean?" he finally said.

I cleared my throat before replying.

"Exactly what I said, Bill. Sean is standing on our lawn. He's looking straight at me. I'm not joking."

The hairs on my arms stood on end and a yearning began to materialize in the pit of my stomach. I could hear Bill sigh on the other end of the line.

"Honey, that's not possible. You know Sean is dead."

The yearning morphed into anger.

"I know that," I spat. "But as real as the cheese sandwiches in your lunch box, Sean is standing on our lawn. I don't know what to do. Am I going insane? Please don't tell me I'm going insane."

I let go of the sheers and pulled my cardigan tighter around me. It had been a difficult year for me, for us, to accept the death of our son. Sean was only seventeen when he was killed by a drunk driver. He had so much life to live yet. There wasn't a day that went by without me wishing it had been me instead of him.

"Maybe it's a prank of one of his friends," Bill said. "Why don't you go outside and talk to him. He may miss him too. It'll be good for you to talk about it with someone."

"Okay," I said, anxiety instantly taking a hold of me. "I'll go and do that. Bye."

"Bye, honey. See you tonight."

I pulled the sheers aside again. Sean was still standing on the lawn. I so wanted it to be Sean. I wanted my son back. I wanted to hold him and cuddle him and tell him I loved him so much. Something kept me from running outside though. There was something about his vision that was unsettling. Bill thought it was a friend of Sean, but I knew Sean's friends. They didn't look like him. This apparition looked like Sean. Hell, it wasn't an apparition. It was Sean. And yet...

With trepidation, I walked to the front door. I put my hand on the doorknob. My breathing increased, and I felt light-headed. I could feel sweat beads forming on the skin of my body. Thinking about the words of my therapist, I tried to control my breathing. I inhaled deeply, releasing the tension slowly with a long exhalation. I did this three times before I had the guts to turn the knob and open the door.

Sean was still standing on the lawn. I pinched the bridge of my nose, closing my eyes. When I opened them again, he was still there, still looking at me.

A feeling of hope crept over me now, the yearning to hold my son again a thousand-fold. I slowly took some steps in his direction. As I did, so did he step away from me. I stopped. He stopped too. I took another few steps. He stepped the same number of steps away from me. What was this boy playing at?

Frowning, I called his name. He didn't react at all. There was no expression on his face. Was Bill right? Was this a prank?

I took some more steps in Sean's direction, but he continued to keep the same distance between us. I became agitated and angry. Why was he not letting me get near him? If anything, I wanted to smack his ear for being so inconsiderate. I began walking fast to him, turning it into a run when Sean began moving away fast too. I was in pursuit for about five minutes, when Sean disappeared into an abandoned house.

I hesitated to follow him in there. I rubbed my neck and looked back. I was out of view of my street, my neighbors. When I looked at the house again, Sean was standing in front of the broken window of the house. I was now the one standing on the lawn, looking at him inside the house. The tables had turned.

Deciding I'd had enough of this cat-and-mouse game, I went inside. When I opened the door into the living room, Sean looked at me and my heart melted when he didn't move away, and I finally saw a smile on his face. I stretched out my arms to embrace my son. Then the world exploded around me.

When I came to, I found myself covered by debris. The house I had been in had collapsed. Fortunately, I had been protected by the door frame and wasn't injured. I managed to climb out of the mess that had been a house just a few minutes ago. The lawn was now covered in debris but not from the house. I saw metal bits, airplane chairs, and a food trolley lying around. I now realized what had happened. A plane had crashed and had leveled part of the neighborhood, including the street I lived in.

I looked back to the flattened house which had shielded me, but Sean was gone. I dropped to my knees, crying as I hugged myself. People ran over to me, asking

me if I was injured. They thought I was in pain. I wasn't.
I was happier than I had ever been, knowing that my son
was my guardian angel.

Alone

Keywords: country, phone, light in trees

It hardly hurt at all. What she felt mostly was the warmness of her blood flowing down her throat and onto her chest. She could still breathe easily as her trachea hadn't been cut. She would be able to live had she been in the position to get to a hospital. As it was, being out in the middle of the night on a dark, country road in the middle of nowhere, that was wishful thinking. She possibly could have called for help, was it not that they had taken her phone. That was the reason they had slit her throat. She had held information on that phone that they wanted. And it had cost her her life.

She dropped to her knees. The gravel pierced her skin, but the blood coming out of her knees was nothing compared with the blood flowing from her carotid artery. Her arms hung limp next to her body. With the medical knowledge she had, she knew that clutching the gaping wound would have absolutely no effect. She was going to die, one way or another. Well, one way, really. No doubt about that.

The perpetrators had not been interested in her at all. It wasn't a personal matter. They had only been interested in the phone, or rather, the data it held and the money they would receive for it. They had left the scene right after wielding the razor-sharp knife and snatching her handbag containing her phone, leaving her to die all alone.

That's what she felt. No pain, no panic. She felt alone. That empty feeling that makes you want to grab your insides and squeeze it in the hope that something will change. In this whole wide world, with billions of people, there was no one here to see her die, no one to see her suffer, no one to hold her hand as she passed to the other side. If there was another side. She would soon know.

Light-headedness made her lose her balance, and she leaned forward on one hand. The blood from her delicate, white neck now flowed directly onto the ground. 'Foxes may come and sniff,' she thought. 'Perhaps lick at her blood, wondering what had happened once her body was discovered and taken away.' She hoped her body would be discovered, and soon. She didn't want to become one of those bloated roadkill corpses you saw deteriorating on the side of the road. Would her abdomen explode at some point? Nausea made her stomach turn. In order to get some fresh air into her lungs, to ease her queasiness, she lifted her head. In the distance, she saw the light of the moon shining through the trees. It was so beautiful. The movement of her head had increased the blood flow and she collapsed onto the ground. As the last of her life's juices left her body, so did her spirit, and there was nothing left but a corpse.

Sisterly Love

Keywords: spoon, make-up artist, Isle of Skye, envy

There they stood, all happy and shining. My sister and her groom. The wedding of the century they called it. Probably true. Who else was going to get married here, in the middle of fucking nowhere? The Isle of Fucking Skye; God's place to torment innocent souls. Right now the rain lashed the town hall as if it wanted to break up the wedding reception inside. The wind was driving it on, howling along with it. It was probably crying with me on this worst day of my life.

My aunt, sitting next to me, had told me to suck it up, to get over my envy. She stopped my hand tapping the dessert spoon on the edge of the table. What did she know? 'Suck it up.' My soulless sister had ruined it all, ruined my life, my happiness. Yet everybody was smiling at her, applauding her words as she gave her speech. I bet she didn't mention how she stole my love away, the conniving bitch that she was. She flashed her pearly white teeth as the lies continued to pour from her mouth. She had always been the pretty one. From when we were toddlers, everybody had always been drawn to her. 'She's so cute,' they'd say. 'What a pretty smile you've got there,' they would croon. No one ever saw me standing there, plain Jane with sleek, mousy-colored hair and a face you would forget as soon as you blinked. Not her. Everybody remembered her. Was it her sky-blue eyes? The dimples in her cheeks as she smiled? She was beautiful, I couldn't deny it. Still, Mum had organized a make-up artist to make her pretty today. As if she needed a fucking make-up artist for her flawless skin. She could make men drool with her looks after she had been boozing all night and having a mother of a hangover. Whatever it was she had, it stole my love from me and she knew it.

It was two years ago that I met him. He was a cousin of the vicar and had come to Skye to help rebuild the church. How handsome he was and so handy with all the tools. We had flirted and teased for weeks. Then, one night after going to the movies, he had kissed me. Me! I had been in seventh heaven. Mum had noticed my happiness and made me spill the beans. I then had to bring him over for dinner of course. That's when my sister got her evil claws into him.

From the moment he saw her, he could only pay attention to her. After all we had shared, the fun, the flirting, the kiss, I suddenly was nothing, an empty space. He listened to every word *she* said, commented on every move *she* made, came to visit *her*. They were always giggling and laughing, no doubt at the expense of me. Soon he was taking *her* to the movies, and kissing *her*.

My aunt looked annoyed at me as I had begun tapping the spoon on the table again. I ignored her. She should know better. She was an old spinster, older sister of my mother, and should know how it felt when your younger sister was getting married before you did. It just wasn't done. My sister, like my mother, had ignored the old tradition. She had taken no heed to my complaints about getting married so soon. And to *him*. She fucking ignored me. Period. So much for sisterly love. Love. It was all a bunch of lies. It only caused grief and pain. My sister hurt me, deeply, yet she didn't give a shit. She had to marry the only man who had looked *my* way, the only man who had kissed *me*. And only because she could. She could get a thousand others to fall in love with her, yet she had to have the one that *I* wanted. She stole him from me, just so she could hurt me, the fucking bitch.

Suddenly, I heard her say, "...and all because of my dear sister." The words were dripping with honey, oozing with feigned love. They made my blood curl and sent shivers down my spine. The people ooh-ed and aah-ed at her words and turned toward me. They didn't know that all she had done was hate me from the moment she was born. Nobody knew she had used every single word, action, and thought to hurt me, to make me feel miserable, worthless, pitied. My rage welled up in me like lava in a volcano. No more!

I turned to her, my eyes blazing a fire from hell. I pulled back my hand and threw the spoon in her direction. It hit the dog that my cousin was playing with in front of the happy couple's table. It yapped in surprise, which made my cousin jump up and fall backward. He tried to keep his balance by holding on to the tablecloth. The wedding cake began shifting as the cloth moved down the table. My love hastened to keep it in place. In his sudden, forceful dive, he slammed down on the edge of the plate holding the cutting knife. The knife flicked up towards his face. He brushed it away with his arm just in time, making it do a somersault high in the air. Lightning reflected off the sharp edge of the blade before the knife went on its downward course. Encountering no resistance, the knife buried itself deep into my sister's heartless chest. The room went quiet. My sister looked at her chest, then at me. She dropped to the floor with only a swishing of her silk, white dress. My love let go of the wedding cake. His eyes were on me.

Finally, I had his attention again.

Reunion

<u>Writing Prompt</u>: They thought I'd forget. But I remembered. Everything.

I pressed the button of the car fob and the blinkers of the gold-colored Ferrari flashed once.

"Wow! Is that your car? Jessica asked. The other two women were too gobsmacked for the moment to say anything, quite an unusual happening for them.

"It sure is. You like it?"

Sherry let her hand glide over the smooth lacquer of the hood, her mouth taking in a breath.

"It's beautiful," she said.

"Are you sure it's yours? You didn't rent or borrow it?" Dana was forever the cool one. The one that told the other two what to think and do. As expected, Sherry immediately took her hands off the car.

"Yes, I'm not having you on. I told you, I've got a pretty good job nowadays."

"Who would have thought..." Jessica said. Her face twitched between pain and admiration as she sat in her wheelchair.

"Let's go for a ride, ladies," I said.

Sherry helped Jessica into the passenger seat, while I handed her wheelchair to one of the doormen at the hotel.

"How did you break your legs, Jess?" Dana asked as she stood by to see Sherry struggle to help Jessica from the wheelchair into the racing seat of the Ferrari.

"It was a hit and run," Jessica panted when she finally sat in the seat. "The car came out of nowhere, hit me full frontal. The driver escaped."

"Did they get him?" Sherry asked.

"Nope, it was a stolen car. I'll never know."

"That sucks," Dana said. The little ray of pitch black.

Sherry and Dana wormed their way into the back seat via the driver's side. I could tell Dana wasn't happy not sitting in the passenger seat, but it would be too socially inept to let a woman with two broken legs wriggle herself in the back seat. Live had finally taught Dana some social graces.

"Where are we going?" Jessica tried to make herself comfortable in the tiny space available to her. The car wasn't designed to carry more than two passengers and there was neither headroom nor legroom to speak of in the back.

"Let's take a drive along the coast," I said. "It's a beautiful drive. You'll love it."

The girls agreed, and I switched on the engine. You could hardly hear it as I exited the driveway of the Hilton.

"So, manager of the big H., eh?" Dana said as soon as we were on our way. "Who did you blow to get that job?"

The Jessica and Sherry suppressed a giggle.

I threw a quick glance at Sherry, then a glance in the rear-view mirror at Dana. "Is it so strange I'm doing well?"

There was a loaded silence in the car.

"Well, considering..." Jessica finally said.

"You mean, how can a girl that was so ugly, stupid, and stuttering all of a sudden look so great, have such an expensive car, and such a good job?"

Sherry dropped her head, blushing out of shame.

"Exactly," Dana said while she stared out of the side window. She still was the same cold-heartedness bitch.

I bit the inside of my lip before I answered. The memories of days gone past rushed in front of my eyes. The times the three of them had called me names, pulled my red hair, thrown the contents of my bag all over the schoolyard. I relived all the times they had made fun of me in front of the whole school, the class, the boys. Emotions welled up. Humiliation, shame, loneliness, hurt. I took a deep breath and straightened myself. I had bested the past. Their terror had hardened me, made me stronger. I had sought comfort in sports. I had become a runner at first, later discovering I had a passion for swimming. Something good had come out of it.

"Call it luck, call it karma, whatever." I refused to tell them how hard I had practiced overcoming my stuttering, how painful the facial reconstruction had been, how hard I had worked to be the best in my field.

"Whatever it was," Jessica said, "I'm glad it worked out for you. I'm not proud of what I... what *we* did to you. It was wrong. I'm so glad you have forgotten all that and organized this reunion." She looked at <u>me</u> but turned away as soon as I met her eyes.

"Yes, we're so glad you've forgotten all that," Sherry said.

"Ditto," Dana added after I spotted Sherry poke her in the ribs.

We chitchatted for a while until the road made a sharp turn. I kept the car going straight ahead. The girls screamed as we crashed through the railing. The car plummeted off the cliff into the sea below. The ocean came closer and closer to the windscreen, Dana began to scream.

"I can't swim! I can't swim!"

"I know," I said.

"Oh my god, get me out. Get me out!" Sherry screamed at the top of her lungs.

"Still claustrophobic?" I asked.

Jessica just sat there, holding on for dear life to her seatbelt. When she looked at me, we both knew that if she managed to get out of the car, her legs casts would drag her to the bottom of the ocean.

As the car hit the water, the airbags inflated. With a pocket knife, I deflated mine and quickly got out of the car as soon as the water pressure would let me. Holding my breath, I turned. Dana and Sherry were both trying to get the driver's seat to move forward, but I had jammed the mechanism with my pocket knife. As soon as they realized they weren't getting out, the three of them looked at me, their eyes bulging as they struggled not to open their mouths. I smiled at them before I swam up for air.

They thought I'd forget.

But I remembered.

Everything.

A Little Indigestion

<u>Keywords</u>: soul, farmer, deal, bathroom

Dave took the last sip of his wine and, although disappointed that the glass was empty, was glad he finally had an excuse to leave. His bladder had been bursting at the seams for the last twenty minutes, but he had been reluctant to leave the gorgeous woman sitting opposite him. Cassandra was everything he had dreamed of. She was pretty, had a good set of brains which she used extremely well, and she liked him. Not a lot of people liked Dave. He was a defense lawyer, defending rapists and murderers. It was a dirty job, but somebody had to do it. It also was a job that never ran out of work and it made good money. Dave put the glass down and looked into the dark eyes of the enchanting beauty opposite him. He put his hand on hers.

"Excuse me, my dear, but I have to visit the bathroom. I'm reluctant to leave your company, but I'm afraid I will embarrass myself if I don't go now. Please don't leave during my temporary absence," Dave said.

"Don't worry, I won't," she answered and bashed her eyelids at him. She took her hand from under his and caressed his. Dave smiled at her.

'We're on a roll,' he thought.

He pushed his chair back and made his way to the restroom of the restaurant. It was a five-star restaurant, one that only high-income earners could afford. Dave never suffered financial problems and had always taken his first dates here. There had been many. Unfortunately, most of them were never up for a second date after he had told them what he did for a living. Cassandra was different though. She also was a defense lawyer, and they had zinged from the moment their eyes met.

Dave entered the restroom and picked the middle stall to relieve himself. As the fluid left his body, relaxation returned to it. When he was done, he zipped up. Before he could turn around to exit the cubicle, a sting of pain went through his chest and up his left arm. Automatically, Dave half collapsed to relieve the pain. Then, it was as if there was a band around his chest being pulled tight. He couldn't breathe. He grabbed at his chest, trying to get rid of the band that wasn't there.

There was a single knock on the cubicle door.

"HELLO," said a voice on the other side.

"Take another cubicle," Dave managed to say while he loosened his tie.

"I'M NOT HERE TO TAKE A PISS," the strange voice said.

'What the fuck?' thought Dave.

"I don't care if you want to do a number two. Just take the cubicle next door."

"I'M NOT HERE TO RELEAVE MYSELF," the voice said again.

Dave was panting. He really wasn't feeling too good.

"Then what are you knocking on my door for? Can't this wait?"

"I THINK THIS IS THE PERFECT MOMENT. MY TIMING IS USUALLY PRETTY GOOD," the stranger continued.

The voice sounded odd, but Dave thought it was due to the blood pressure rising in his ears.

"What do you want, man? What are you?" he said. He was sweating like he was running a fever now. He leaned against the wall of the cubicle. Hopefully getting some weight off his legs would help make him feel better.

"YOU COULD SAY I'M A FARMER," the stranger said.

'A farmer?' thought Dave. 'Farmers don't earn enough to be able to afford to eat here.'

"Fuck off!" Dave said. Another shoot of pain seared through his chest. "Aargh!"

"I'M SORRY, IT USUALLY IS AN INCONVENIENT TIME, BUT HARVEST TIME IS HERE."

There was no humor, no sarcasm in the voice, and through the spasms of pain, Dave was wondering what mushrooms this guy had been eating. He would have to look at the restaurant menu a bit better next time.

"I'M THE GRIM REAPER. I'M HERE TO TAKE YOUR SOUL," the stranger said.

"Look, I'm not in the mood for Halloween jokes. It's still September for fuck's sake." Dave took a few more shallow breaths. Suddenly, a hooded head appeared through the cubicle door. Dave couldn't see the face as the shadow inside the hood was too dark.

"What the fuck?" he managed. He straightened up a little, trying to get as far away as possible from the apparition. A new pain-wave tortured his body, and he doubled up.

"I REALLY AM SORRY ABOUT THE TIMING, BUT YOU ARE DYING AND I'M HERE TO TAKE YOUR SOUL," Death said looking down at Dave.

Thoughts raced through Dave's mind. 'Dying? Dying? It's just a bit of indigestion, heartburn. I don't want to die now. Cassandra's waiting for me. I haven't had a fuck in ages and my chances have never been better for getting laid.' The pain subsided again, and Dave straightened himself carefully.

"Okay, I get it. You reap souls. That's your job. How about I give you three instead of my single one?" Dave said.

"THAT'S NOT HOW IT WORKS. THERE ARE RULES," Death said, now standing next to Dave in the small space of the cubicle.

"Rules are there to be broken, everybody knows that," Dave responded and looked Death straight in the eye. Well, where he thought Death's eyes should be.

With a bony hand, Death stroked the presumed location of his chin.

"NOBODY EVER TOLD ME. SOUNDS GREAT. TELL ME MORE."

"I'm a defense lawyer. I'm defending three guys on death row at the moment. I could get them out with ease, but if I make them lose the trial, they'll be executed, and you'll have three souls to reap. Don't tell me you don't like that. What do you say? Is it a deal? You'll only get this deal today, you know."

Dave stuck his hand out to Death. Death didn't move.

"Going once, going twice..."

Death hesitated at first but finally shook Dave's hand. Dave thought it felt unreal and cold.

"DEAL," Death said and disappeared into nothing.

Dave took a deep breath and felt his chest muscles relax. He left the cubicle, washed his hands, and straightened his tie.

Back in the restaurant, Cassandra asked what took him so long.

"Sorry, I had to close a deal. Now, where were we?"

They had a great evening and Dave made love to Cassandra that night as if there was no tomorrow.

High

Writing Prompt: A story about fame

The wind blew through Jason's hair. He felt so high at the moment and not only because of the dose of uppers he had just taken. Jason looked down and saw the crowd below him. It always gave him a tremendous rush to stand in front of his audience.

He had come a long way these last five years. It had begun with his Year 11 stage performance as Tony in the musical 'West Side Story.' His singing had piqued the interest of a parent in the audience. The man had appeared to be in the singing business and had taken him apart after the performance. "You have a future there, kid," he had said. "With your voice and your looks, you can conquer the world." The words had been music to Jason's ears. His parents were thrilled as well as Jason hadn't shown much interest in his future so far and certainly didn't have the brain capacity to study. They had taken the man's business card with gratitude and within a week, Jason had an appointment for an interview.

It had all been a rollercoaster ride from then on, a thrill ride that most kids could only dream of. He had been put into contests, the most profitable one being 'America's Got Talent.' He had won it, and the fame that came with it was overwhelming, to say the least. Since then, he had made several albums, done a tour of America, and had recently finished a world tour. Not that he had seen much of the world. The inside of hotel rooms doesn't show you much of the culture of a country other than what brand of whiskey they favor. The most he had seen of the countries he had visited had been from an airplane or a taxi window. There had definitely not been much time for sightseeing. The times he had ventured out and about had been for photo shoots and there was not much pleasure in that.

There had been girls though. 'Ah, the girls,' Jason thought. His memory visited the many girls he had been with. They had all given their bodies so freely to him, including the diseases that those bodies carried. He had learned his lesson soon enough and carried condoms with him wherever he went now. He put his hand in his pocket and touched one of the little square packages. 'Don't leave home without it,' Jason thought with a smile. He looked down at the crowd. It was a mixed crowd this time, but there were always the girls, swooning and shrieking. He stepped forward and put both his arms up in the air. The crowd roared. How he loved that sound. Did he see one of the girls faint? Possibly. Very likely actually, they always did.

Jason looked up into the night sky. It looked so peaceful. It was the quiet before the storm. Soon, he would give the performance of a lifetime. He was pepped up and ready.

It was one of the early lessons he had learned from his manager. "Always please your audience," she had said. "No matter what you do, never disappoint your audience. Without them, you are nothing." Jason had memorized those words as if they were written in the bible. He had played the crowds, pleased them, gave them the performance of a lifetime. Every. Single. Time. Wherever he went, his fans always came first. His manager had tried to stop him signing autographs so many times when they were on their way to a concert or an interview, but Jason had never listened, always making time for his fans. It was part of his attraction to them. He gave his fans the feeling they meant something to him. So many famous persons didn't care about their fans. At least, they didn't show it. And their fan base would shrink because of it. Not Jason's. Jason felt he could rule the world if his fans wanted him to. He certainly would have enough voters to with a presidential election.

Jason stepped up to the edge of the stage. The crowd below went wild. He ran to the left, and the crowd to the left roared. He ran to the right, and the crowd to the right roared. Blood pumped through Jason's veins, delivering the adrenaline to every single cell in his body. He casually walked back to the center. There, he turned to face his fans. He put his feet together in a dramatic way while stretching out his arms. Again, the crowd went wild. He put both hands to his mouth and threw a kiss into the crowd. Girls were definitely fainting now. He felt better than he ever felt before. Slowly, he stretched his arms out sideways again.

A single noise rang out. Jason's body moved back a split second. He staggered backward but immediately stepped forward again. He wasn't going to lose his center spot on the stage now. Jason looked down. There was a patch of red on his shirt that was growing bigger. As he felt a weakness come over him, accompanied by a clammy feeling, he took a step forward. There was nothing for his foot to stand on and he fell. The wind through his hair felt refreshing. The roar of the crowd was deafening. This was what it was all about. This was what he had lived for all his life. As he fell from the six-story building's rooftop, he caught a glimpse of the rifle on the rooftop opposite that had fired the fatal bullet. Faster and faster Jason fell. It seemed to take forever. Jason's eyes took in the crowd as they drew nearer. He smiled at them. So this was his final performance. He was going to die young, so he would always be young and beautiful in his fans' eyes.

The assassin who had wielded the rifle was packing up to make a quick getaway. This had been his weirdest assignment ever. It paid well, he didn't complain about that. Nor was the request a difficult one. His client had let him know where and when the target would be available. Figuring out where to position himself and sorting out which rifle to use had been a piece of cake. It had been weird because he never had someone order a hit on himself.

When Jason's body finally hit the pavement, his fame skyrocketed.

Three Men on a Bench

<u>Writing Assignment</u>: A story about three different
characters

There was a bench in the park, on top of the hill, where
the treetops gave way to a stunning view over the town.
It was a wanted spot by all who use the park. Many
marriages had been proposed here. Some men had
gotten a positive answer, some not. One of the lucky
ones now sat on the bench, alone. While he enjoyed the
view, his memory took him back to the good old days he
spent here courting his recently deceased wife.

"George! Fancy meeting you here!" a voice called
out.

George was taken out of his daydream and turned his
head and upper body to find out who was talking to
him. His joints weren't as mobile as they used to be
anymore.

"Dicky? Is that you? What the devil are you doing
here?" George hadn't seen Dicky for years.

"Yes, it's me. What a coincidence meeting you here."
Dicky walked up to George with a spring in his step.

George tried to stand up to greet Dicky, but pain
shot through his back. He let himself fall back onto the
bench.

"Ouch! Sorry, old man, a handshake will have to do."

"Speak for yourself," said Dicky as he took George's hand and bent down to give his old friend a man-hug. "I don't consider myself an old man. I'm only seventy-two and as fit as a fiddle. What happened to you?" Dicky wiped the bench next to George, pinched the front of his trousers, and pulled them up as he sat down next to George. His eyes swept the view and glazed over as he, too, was momentarily taken back in time by memories.

"Oh, life. The usual. Working as a brickie isn't kind on your body, you know." Dicky nodded, and George wondered what had kept Dickie so fit. "What have you been up to? The last thing I heard was that you left for France." George changed position slightly, so he could at least see a bit of Dicky as they talked. With his hands he steadied himself on the bench, so his body didn't automatically turn back to the looking-forward looking position.

Dickie put one leg over the other and clasped his hands over his knee.

"France was just the beginning. You name it, I've been there. I could tell you what I've seen, but I don't think we have the time."

"I've got plenty of time," George said. "My Nettie died last month. Cancer. Nasty business. Now she's gone, I seem to have more time than I can fill."

Tears welled up in George's eyes. He looked away and first wiped his nose before he casually wiped the tear that escaped his left eye. Dicky pretended he hadn't seen it.

"So sorry to hear that, George. Nettie was a great woman and, I bet, a great wife."

"What about you? Did you ever marry? George asks.

"No, no. I never felt the need to settle down. Too much to see and do, too many women to taste." He smiled and nudged George with his elbow. George smiled back.

From a distance, they heard a muttering coming closer. It appeared to be a man walking his dog. The dog wasn't on the lead and the man seemed to be trying to get the dog to come to him.

"Here, boy. Here! Bloody mutt. Come here, I say." The dog thought the man was playing a game and every time the man moved to get the lead onto the dog's collar, it moved out of reach.

"What do you know. Isn't that Beaky Bernard?" Dicky said to George.

Dicky leaned forward and squinted. When the man with the lead got near enough, he recognized him as well.

"It sure is," George said. "I recognize that nose in a million."

They both laugh. Beaky Bernard, with his bird-like nose, had always been the class clown.

"Bernard, fancy meeting you here," Dicky said when Bernard was closer.

The man chasing the dog, wearing a tweed jacket and hat, and leather boots, looked up at the men sitting on the bench.

"Dicky and George. Well, what do you know? What on earth are you two doing in this godforsaken place?"

"What do you mean?" said George. "It's quite beautiful up here."

The two men shuffled down one end of the bench to make space for Bernard.

"I'm not going to sit on that piece of junk," Bernard said. Dicky looked at George and back to Bernard.

"It's okay, man. We won't eat you." Dickie patted the empty bench next to him.

"Oh, alright. This dog has taken nearly all the breath out of me."

The dog, a black Labrador, was running around the men, chasing birds and diving for insects in the grass.

"He's a cutie. What's his name?" George asked.

"Blackie. His name is Blackie," Bernard answered.

"How original. Did you choose it?" Dicky said. Bernard glanced through narrowed eyes to Dicky, whose face remained a picture of friendliness.

"What are you two faggots doing up here anyway?" Bernard said to the two men. "Did the institution have a power failure?"

Both men chuckle, glad Beaky Bernard hadn't lost his way with words.

"Actually, I'm here on a date." Dicky nodded toward a woman walking up the path. She's tall, moving gracefully. As she came nearer, her delicate facial features became visible. She was in her fifties, but still a looker. The three men feasted their eyes on her appearance.

"Well, well, well. You sexy devil. Haven't lost your touch, have you?" Bernard muttered. "Better make sure you've got some rubber on you. You can catch nasty things these days."

George made a serious effort to get up now. With some help from Dicky, he managed to get to his feet.

"Gentlemen, it was a pleasure to meet you. I hope we can do it again some time." George tapped his head in a short salute. "Come on, Beaky. Let's give the two turtle doves some space."

"Alright, alright. I know when I'm not wanted." Bernard rose and followed George down the path, cursing as Blackie still refused to come near him.

Connection

<u>Writing Assignment</u>: A story about a missed
connection and its consequences

Jay Starkey checked his data. He ran his hand through
his hair and licked his lips.

"Holy Shit," he said under his breath.

He typed in a renewed command and checked the
resulting data on his computer again. When the same
results rolled over his screen, he sat back, staring at his
computer. Nothing changed for a few moments.

Suddenly, Jay noticed the time display in the
righthand corner of his computer screen.

"Fuck, fuck, fuck!" he said to himself as he jumped
up and grabbed his jacket. He was nearly out the door
when he halted. He ran back to this computer and hit
the print button. Slowly, the printer started up, making
its rattling noises.

"Come on. Hurry up, you stupid slow thing!" Jay was
not a person to be easily phased, but this was a crucial
moment and time was of the essence. He was an
astronomer, paid by NASA to do some research on a
nearby, possibly habitable planet. He wasn't earning big
bucks with it, but it paid the bills and kept him off the
streets. Nobody thought he would actually come up
with something. It was more a courtesy to his professor

at Stanford University who had mentioned the potential of Jay to his peers at NASA that got him hired.

When the paper rolled out of the machine, Jay's heart sank. He had forgotten to change the ink cartridge last time when he had noticed the machine was running out of ink. He yanked the machine open and pulled the empty cartridge from its belly. He chucked it over his shoulder, not taking note of the stains it made when it hit the carpet. Yanking open at least three drawers of his desk, he found the new cartridge and frantically tried to open it.

"Fuck, fuck, fuckerdyfuck!" he yelled, now looking through his drawers for scissors to open the hard-plastic cover containing the cartridge.

When he finally had the printer going again, the so desired results of his calculations appeared black on white and it took a tremendous effort on Jay's behalf not to yank the paper out of the slow machine too early. He folded the paper and stuffed it into the pocket of his jacket while he ran to his car. Hitting the gas pedal like Dominic Toretto, the car sped out of Saturn Drive.

"Steve, this is Jay. I need you to stop the landing!" Jay knew it was illegal to use his cell phone while driving, but this was a matter of life and death. "Steve, can you hear me? You're breaking up!"

Jay looked at his cell for a split second and saw that the reception icon was not showing any bars.

"Motherfucking useless piece of shit!" He threw his cell onto the passenger seat and pressed his foot on the gas pedal a little further to the floor.

It didn't take long before a flashing light appeared in Jay's rearview mirror and a police vehicle ordered him to pull over. Jay thought for a split second on what to do. He could drive on and risk a hefty fine after being gunned down by police, or pull over and convince the police officer to give him a police escort.

The police officer sauntered over to Jay's vehicle.

"Come on, hurry up!" Jay said under his breath while maintaining his hands on his steering wheel.

"License, please," the officer said when he had reached Jay's window.

Jay pulled out his wallet and gave the officer his license card.

"Officer, I am an astronomer working for NASA and I have vital information regarding a landing that they need to have as soon as possible. Can you please help me get there in time?" Sweat was now forming on Jay's brow.

The officer looked at Jay through his reflective glasses. "We'll see," was all he said, and he sauntered back to his vehicle. There, he reached into his car and as he leaned on the door frame, he began talking through his radio.

Jay drummed his fingers on the steering wheel. He noted his cell and grabbed it again. Still no reception.

He really needed to get a better provider. Trying to find the police officer in his side mirror, his heart stopped for a moment when the man suddenly appeared beside him.

"You seem to be legit. Follow me," he said. Jay let out a sigh of relief.

The officer pulled out in front of Jay, siren blasting. Jay followed him as close as he could. The ride was fast and without further delays. When they reached the gates of the Johnson building, the police vehicle pulled to the side and Jay made a quick salute as he passed the police officer.

Ned, NASA's gatekeeper, let Jay through without a hindrance and Jay sped to the building's entrance where he left the car open and running. He raced through the corridors of the building. Out of breath, he stumbled into the mission control room.

Steve stood looking at the center big screen. He had one arm resting on his ample belly, the fingers of his other hand pinching his lips. Everyone in the room was watching the center screen on which only static was visible. The tension in the room was almost palpable.

"Steve, you've got to stop the landing!" Jay yelled as he made his way to Steve. He had taken the piece of paper from his pocket and pushed it under Steve's nose. Steve took the piece of paper and unfolded it.

"Why?" he asked.

"Because they'll die if you don't. We may all die if you don't," Jay said. He flumped into a chair and looked up at Steve. His lungs were burning as if someone had poured acid into them.

"You're too late," Steve said. "The landing has just begun. They're currently entering the atmosphere and we have to wait until they reach the surface before we have contact again." Steve now read what was on the piece of paper. "Is this a joke?" he asked Jay, who sat with his face in his hands.

"No, it's not. It's a translation of a signal I picked up from the planet," Jay said. His voice was hardly audible.

"What's does it say?" asked Steve's assistant. Steve sighed and read the text out loud.

"Resistance is futile. You will be assimilated."

How Deep Is Your Love?

<u>Writing Assignment</u>: Bring out an emotion

I'm standing at the sink doing the dishes and the song 'How Deep Is Your Love' by the Bee Gees comes up on the radio. I look up and out of the window, staring at nothing in particular. God, this song takes me back. Immediately I think of your blue eyes and how they sparkled, so full of life and energy. I think of those eyelashes, long and dark, surrounding them. They were like an aura around your soul. How I wished those eyes had looked at me the way I had looked at them. I loved looking at you so much.

Now I think of it, it's funny how we grew up together, from Kindy to Year 6, and how I never felt about you before like the way I did when I was twelve. All of a sudden you were all that existed. Nobody else mattered so much in my life as you did for me at that time. I can't remember what it was that made me feel this way; a glance in my direction, a kind word, or perhaps a touch. I truly can't remember. Whatever it was, you got me hooked and each day, I loved you more.

I loved the way you shook your head to get your blond fringe out of your eyes. I loved the way your cheeks and nose turned red when the weather was cold. I loved your little snort of a laugh. I loved the way you strutted across the schoolyard, so self-assured, so different from me.

Seeing you walking across the schoolyard in my mind's eye makes me smile again.

Everybody loved you. They looked up to you, revered you. And why not? You were handsome and clever. You stood up for your beliefs and for others. Everybody laughed when you said something funny. Everybody listened when you said something serious. You were always the center of attention, and nobody minded. Everybody wanted to be you. I wanted to be with you.

I pick up another plate and put it in the soapy water.

My love for you became so great, that one day I was bold enough to ask you for a photograph. To my surprise, you gave me one the next day. At the time I didn't wonder where you got it from so fast, even though it was the pre-digital era. Now I wonder if you had photographs lying around to hand out to swooning girls. I didn't think about that at the time, too overjoyed with your photo. In it, you were wearing a yellow-blue striped polo-shirt, had your arms folded, and sported that cheeky smile of yours. When I came home that day, I immediately framed the photo and put it next to my bed.

Automatically, I turn my head towards my bedroom upstairs. There, on my nightstand are two photos. One taken on my wedding day and one of my children taken last Christmas. I smile again.

For months I kissed you goodnight every night. I would look at your photo and this feeling would wash over me, very much like an ache. How I yearned to be with you, how I wanted to feel your touch, how I wanted for you to know how much I loved you. I can almost feel that feeling again. It's only a few millimeters away from me, and I stretch myself to the limit to touch it, but it's just out of reach. No matter how much I try, as if I really know how to, I can't make that feeling come back. This brings on another kind of ache, and I sigh as I put a clean plate on the drying rack and pick up a dirty one.

As you gave no hint of your feelings towards me after I asked you for the photograph, I realized I had to ask you in a more 'direct' way. So I recorded a cassette tape with songs from the radio. The first song was 'How Deep Is Your Love' by the Bee Gees, the one that still plays in the background. It also had 'You're The One That I Want' from the movie 'Grease' and 'Endless Love' sung by Diana Ross and Lionel Ritchie on it, amongst others with suggestive titles.

My dishwashing brush goes round and round over the plate, like the needle over an LP as I try to recall all the songs I recorded. I remember at least five. When I can't think of any more, I put the plate on the rack.

I never gave you the tape. You never told me how deep your love for me was. You never told me you loved me. When Year 6 ended, we went our own ways, and I never saw you again. My parents had ambitions for me and sent me to a school in the city. You went to the local high school. I never knew what became of you. I hoped to get a glimpse of you at school reunions, but you were never there. Some said you had joined the army and had moved away. Others said that you had settled down and had a family now, leading a quiet life.

I find myself staring out of the window again.

Whatever you are doing, I hope you are happy. I am happily married now. I have a loving husband and we have three beautiful children together. Honestly, I am happy, and I wouldn't want my life to be any other way. But sometimes, some days, at moments like these, I wished I had that feeling like I had for you, that feeling that plucked every single heartstring and reverberated through to my bone marrow. A love so deep, it feels like the essence of my existence. Sometimes, I wished I had that feeling once again.

Cou de Canard

<u>Keywords</u>: a meticulous engineer, Paris, propeller, duck

Sophie entered the boutique-type restaurant in Quartier Latin, Paris, as Pierre held the door open for her. She had met Pierre online and, as they were both single, after a few weeks of amicable, digital communication they had agreed to meet in person. Pierre had suggested having dinner at the little restaurant; neutral territory. Sophie had agreed, although she didn't know the restaurant. But that was the point.

As she passed Pierre with some difficulty, she wasn't the slimmest thirty-two-year-old, she gave him a quick smile and looked away a bit too soon. She blushed as she realized this and kept her fingers crossed inside her coat pocket in the hope he hadn't noticed. Pierre's physical form didn't appear to be what she had imagined when she had chatted with him online. In her mind's eye, he had been abundantly muscled and deadly handsome. Instead, he seemed skinny and was nearly bald. As she was looking down, she noticed his large feet. Even the sides of his shoes were hanging over the end of the soles and were worn.

A waiter interrupted her thoughts.

"Your coats, please," he said.

Pierre helped Sophie out of her coat, but when he wanted to hand it to the waiter she took it from him and folded the coat neatly before handing it over. Pierre frowned but shrugged without saying a word as they followed another waiter to a table. As Pierre moved, Sophie couldn't help but notice that his butt was big. He was skinny overall but had a big butt. 'What a strange body shape,' she thought.

The waiter pulled out a chair for Sophie and Pierre sat down opposite her. The waiter asked what they wanted to drink as he handed them the menu. Pierre was given the wine list.

The table had wobbled when they sat down. Sophie took both corners in her hand and, rocking the table, measured how much one of the legs was lifted from the ground.

"Sophie?" Pierre said.

She looked up and saw Pierre indicating the waiter.

"Madam, what would you like to drink," the waiter repeated. Sophie had been too obsessed with the wobbly table to notice the first time he asked. She noticed Pierre's raised eyebrow and upturned corner of his mouth.

"Oh, sorry, yes. Um, what are you having, Pierre?"

"I'm going for a Riesling wine," he said.

"But that's a dessert wine," Sophie exclaimed.

"That may be so, but I fancy one now," Pierre smiled. It was one of the character traits that Sophie had liked about him when they had chatted online. He didn't seem to care about what others thought about him. She had a quick glance at the wine list that he had passed to her.

I prefer to have a Pinot Noir, the Domaine du Cros lo Sang del Pais Marcillac, please," Sophie said as she handed the wine list back to the waiter.

"That sounds delicious, I think I'll have that one too instead," Pierre said to the waiter as Sophie handed the man the wine list. The waiter left to fulfill their order.

"You know your wines," Pierre mused.

"It's a wine from the Aveyron area. Their wines are indeed delicious," Sophie replied. "Do you have a business card?"

Pierre blinked and for a moment his mouth fell open. "I... didn't think this was going to be a business meeting," he said but did pull his wallet out.

"It's not, but I gave my last card away this afternoon and haven't had the time to fill my card holder yet."

Pierre looked on in wonder as Sophie took his card, folded it double twice, and ducked underneath the table. When she resurfaced again she put both her hands flat on the table.

"There, now it's not wobbly anymore," she said with a smile. "I can't stand wobbly tables."

Pierre's eyes had a twinkle that she couldn't place. She was distracted by the waiter again, who brought them their wines.

"Here's to engineering, what brought us together," Pierre said as he held up his glass.

"You're not an engineer," Sophie said and hesitated to put her glass against that of Pierre.

"Correct, but that's not what I said. What I meant was that if you hadn't been an engineer, I wouldn't have sent you that email about my plane's propeller, we wouldn't have started chatting, and we certainly wouldn't have been sitting in this cozy restaurant having a lovely glass of wine from the Aveyron area together."

Sophie dipped her head slightly with a blush and clinked her glass against his before they both took a sip.

"A very nice wine indeed," Pierre said before he put his glass down.

As Sophie was still too embarrassed about her continuous stream of blunders, she picked up the menu and hid behind it. After a little while of reading in silence, Pierre put down his menu.

"Do you know yet what starter you're going for?"

Sophie looked up when Pierre asked his question. She couldn't help but notice Pierre's neck. It was long and angled, like that of a cartoon duck, with the sticking out Adam's apple that bobbed up and down as he spoke.

"Cou de canard," she murmured.

"Excellent choice! I think I'm going for Foie Gras."

Pierre looked intensely at Sophie as he said it. She sat staring back at him for a moment. Then they burst out laughing together. The rest of their evening was a very pleasant one, with plenty more wine from the Aveyron area.

The Curse

Keywords: Ghost story, female, ship, trunk

1841

The storm was savage.

"Shorten the main course!" Captain Martinez yelled at the crew of the Trouvadore, trying to get his voice to rise above the raging wind.

They were being blown off course and treacherously close to the reef off Breezy Point. They needed to claw the ship clear of the rocks, and fast. He'd already given the order to shorten the top-sails and top-gallants of the fore, but he knew it wasn't enough. "Hurry up, you lazy, rotten mongrels!" He raised his cat-o'-nine-tails and flayed the closest person he could find.

His journey was almost over. The crossing had gone as good as could be expected. They had managed to cross the Atlantic unnoticed by the British Navy patrols. Slavery had been abolished by the Brits several years ago, but that's what made this trip so profitable. The Cubans needed slaves on their sugar cane plantations and the ones he had stored below deck were a fine lot. He'd lost more crew on the way over to Africa than he'd lost slaves coming back. Nobody said it was an easy way to make money, but he'd do well after being paid for this expedition. Maybe he would settle down with a nice, warm, white wife.

As he abused some more crew members verbally and physically, his thoughts flashed back to that black wench he had in his cabin the other day. His eye had fallen on her as soon as she had stepped aboard his ship. She was a beauty, with strong limbs and beautiful teeth. And those lips! The memory of the things he had made her do with those made him harden again. Then the stupid witch had made demands. Who did she think she was? She was a slave and was in no position to make demands. The scurvy bitch demanded better food and treatment for 'her blacks.' The whore! He had beaten her near to death, the only reason these creatures understood.

When she finally was able to get up off his cabin floor, she had cursed him and his family. She had taken the wooden statue from his desk and had done some mumbo-jumbo dancing around it. He had bought the statue from the slave owner in Africa. It was a lovely statue of a woman with huge breasts and a big butt. He liked his women that way. Now she was defiling it with her voodoo magic. One more blow to her head had shut her up. That had taught her who was master. He had locked the statue in his trunk and thrown the woman on his bed before having his way with her again.

Martinez chuckled as he adjusted his package in his trousers. The smile on his face disappeared when he heard the hull of the Trouvadore shatter on the reef. The ship fell off to leeward, making the waves come crashing over the deck. Wails rose from below.

"Cut the blacks loose! Go, before they drown, you son of a whore!" Martinez shouted to his bosun. His stare followed the back of the man as the bosun hurried off. He then looked around the dramatic scene, the white of his eyes matching the white of the waves crashing onto the deck. He'd been so close! East Caicos was British territory and not a good place to strand. He was sure he'd had to deal with that soon, but there was no point in worrying what could happen if none of them survived.

Fortunately, the ship had stranded on a shallow reef close to the beach. When the blacks were out of their shackles, crew and cargo climbed over the lee side into the shallows of the bay. Martinez was the captain, but no way on earth would he stay on the ship last and face the possibility of drowning. He worked against the tide through the chest high crashing surf and made it to shore. Like a half-drowned cat, he fell to his knees, desperately catching his breath. Like him, many others made it to shore. Drenched, drained of energy, they fell onto the sand, praying to their gods they had survived.

Martinez turned around to find his crew. He saw movement from the corner of his eye. Some of the blacks were trying to escape, running the length of the beach. He opened his leather pouch and pulled out his pistol. Quickly loading the weapon, he aimed and fired. One of the blacks went down. It made the others stop in their tracks. Martinez sent his first and second mate over to retrieve the slaves. When they dropped the body of the slave that had fallen at his feet, Martinez recognized her as the woman who had cursed him.

"Poxy whore," he muttered as he kicked sand over her dead body. He would have gotten a fair price for one as pretty as her.

"Oi, you there!"

Martinez looked around to find where the voice came from and found locals had surrounded them on the dunes enclosing the beach, holding muskets and pistols aimed at him and his crew.

"Rotten landlubbers," Martinez swore as he and his crew were taken into custody.

2004

They had predicted a storm coming, but there was still time to make one more dive. The team was very excited they had found what they thought to be the Trouvadore, the Spanish two-master that had taken slaves from Africa to the Spanish territory of Cuba illegally, years after the treaty between Spain and Britain that abolished slavery. The story of the ship was a great one as it was rumored that 193 slaves had survived the shipwreck and, as slavery was outlawed on the island, they were all freed. Now they hoped to find the remains of the ship near the shores of East Caicos, where wooden remains had been found.

Derrek checked the scuba gear of his dive buddy, Luke. Luke did the same for him, and when they both had checked their wrist computers which told them they had enough air for about forty minutes, they jumped from the ship into the warm waters off Breezy Point. As they surfaced, they made the divers' sign for 'okay' to the boat crew, exchanged their snorkels for the regulators and disappeared under the water's surface.

Derrek and Luke were both archaeologists. They had met by chance during their scuba training course and had been diving together since. Shipwrecks were their favorites, and to be asked by the Smithsonian to help find the Trouvadore was an offer they couldn't refuse. They had gone over the letters that had surfaced about the alleged ship and had done some digging in archives to find out as much as possible.

"Hey, the captain's name is Martinez," Luke had said to Derrek as he was reading one of the logs from the Smithsonian archives.

"You're kidding?" Derrek said as he looked up from the paper he was researching. "Really?"

"Yes, really. It says so here. Captain: Alvarez Maria Guan Martinez," Luke read aloud from the paper.

"Wow, he could be my ancestor. My father always said we had sailor's blood in our veins. Remind me to look into that when we get back. Dad often mentioned we had a curse put on our family, but nothing interesting ever happened to any of our relatives as far as we know. This could be it though."

"Sure, Maria, but you know as well as I do that Captain Martinez didn't die when the ship went down," Luke grinned.

"Shut it, that's a perfectly normal Spanish name for a boy. They're very catholic over there."

"If you say so, Maria."

"Oh, shut it, I said!" Derrek kicked Luke in the shins and they had continued their research in silence.

They swam through the silent waters off Breezy Point until they came upon what they thought was the wreck of the Trouvadore. You had to have some imagination to see it as a ship. It was covered in barnacles and corals, but to Derrek and Luke it was clear from the moment they saw it that this was not a naturally formed coral reef. Beautiful colored fish hid amongst its skeleton. Derrek and Luke looked at each other and both made the 'O' signal at the same time. 'Jinx' thought Derrek. He wanted to smile, but that was hard to do with a regulator in your mouth.

They circled the wreck, hoping to get an indication of its age or what sort of a ship it had been. They became sure it had been a two-master, which matched the description of what they had found during their research of the Trouvadore. When they swam over the wreck, Derrek saw an opening. He took out a metal pointer and tapped it on his scuba tank. Luke heard the noise and turned around. Derrek pointed downwards to the hole in the reef. Luke's eyes grew big and he made the 'O' signal before adjusting his BCD to go deeper. They both had come prepared with nets and lights. They, of course, also had knives strapped to their legs, just in case they met inquisitive sharks.

As soon as they entered the hull of the ship, they switched on their lights, mounted on their heads like true speleologists. In the depth of the ship, they found more barnacles, more coral, and structures that looked like platforms. As they found the rusted remains of iron shackles on the platforms, the both of them became ecstatic, knowing that they had found what they were looking for, the slave ship Trouvadore.

The slave trade hadn't been a pleasure cruise for the slaves as their captors had tried to pack as many slaves as possible onto their ships, packed shoulder to shoulder, without enough space above them to even turn around. Seeing the proof of these torturous circumstances made shivers go down Derrek's spine. So much so, that he became unwell. Derrek didn't know why, but he wanted to get out. He was breathing faster than normal and couldn't think straight. He was having a panic attack. This was very unusual for Derrek, having a long list of wreck dives to his name, which made him panic even more. He grabbed Luke by a fin and pointed towards the exit. Luke nodded and followed him.

Derrek almost got out when something kept him from going forward. His heart skipped a beat and he almost stopped breathing. Turning around as fast as he could, he relaxed when he saw it was Luke holding him by his fins. Luke pointed at another hole in the wreck. Derrek consulted his computer and realized they had enough time for some more exploration. The idea he was getting out had made his breathing slow down. He had bested the attack and rationalized he should be okay. He didn't want to disappoint Luke as they may not have another chance to dive for another few days with this storm soon upon them.

Derrek nodded and followed Luke into the hole. This had to be the captain's quarters, or what was left of it, according to the maps they had studied. There wasn't much left of it. One object that had been preserved in miraculously good condition was a chest. As soon as Luke saw it, he swam to it and opened it, greed the main motivator. Derrek felt the hairs on his body rise under his dive suit.

From around the chest swam a barracuda which attacked Luke's face. His mask was ripped off, his regulator hose torn. There was blood everywhere. Derrek was petrified, unable to move, but not because of what happened to Luke. The cause of his fear was coming from within the chest. In it was a wooden statue in the shape of a voluptuous woman. It wasn't the statue that frightened him. It was the ghostlike shimmer that rose from it. The ghost didn't disappear. It hovered just above the chest and looked straight at Derrek. It. Stared. At. Him. Then it began laughing. There was no sound, but the image of the ghost laughing at him made his heart stop and blood drain from his head. This was the curse put on his family. It had been trapped, but now it was free. Derrek moved backward as fast as he could. He bumped into the back of the cabin wall. The move damaged the first stage of his regulator. All the air in his tank escaped with forceful bubbles.

The last thing Derrek saw through the red waters was the laughing ghost disappearing from the ship, finally having her revenge, finally free.

Hunting

Keywords: Suspense, Romance, Diary, Duck

He pulled their Land Rover Evoque out of the driveway.

"Who's Clive?" John said.

Fuck, how did he find out about Clive?

"He's the artist I commissioned to paint the painting I gave you for your fiftieth birthday. Why do you ask?"

"I found your diary."

"You read my fucking diary?"

Bloody hell, did he read it all?

"Yes, I did. And just in case you're wondering, yes, I did read it all."

"For fuck's sake, John, that stuff is personal. Diaries normally are."

I took a deep breath, crossed my arms, and stared out of the side window.

"Is it true though? Do you really hate me that much?" John asked. I threw him a quick glance and saw he was waiting for my answer.

John and I had been married for over thirty years now. His family had money and John had been considered a great catch. He had been smitten with me, falling head over heels for the blonde, knockout girl. And I had gladly taken the opportunity to make a better future for myself.

At first, I had been in seventh heaven with John spoiling me with jewelry and attention. But the attention soon dwindled as work became more important than being with me. The jewelry offers also declined over time, although he had been giving me the odd piece now and again to stop me from whining. Kids had kept me happy, but they had moved out years ago and I had been deprived of love again. I had kept myself busy with going to the spa once a month, having my hair and nails done every fortnight, and having a massage every week. The girls I hang out with were in the same boat as me and as we spent our husbands' money, we moaned about the loveless lives we lived.

That changed when I met Clive. Clive was an artist and he caught my attention at a friend's birthday party when he spoke so passionately about his profession. I had asked him to paint a large hunting scene, to be the centerpiece of our hallway, as a display of the love John and I shared for hunting. Clive was all too happy to give me the attention I so craved for. And so I visited him more and more frequently, to check up on the painting's progress of course. But one thing led to another and before I knew it we were having an affair.

"Well, you're not flowing over with passion for me anymore. What did you expect?" I said after about a minute.

John didn't react, as usual.

After a few minutes of silence, he pointed into the air straight ahead and said, "Look, ducks. I hope we shoot some ducks today."

That was John's greatest tactic. Redirection of attention.

We drove on in silence for another twenty minutes before John veered the car onto the off ramp and parked it in the little car park next to the highway. From there we would walk to our usual hunting ground. We got out, and I opened the back of the car. Sootie, our black Labrador, jumped out and started running around me in circles from excitement as John got our rifles out of the car. I preferred my A300 Outlander over John's Remington 870, as it was so much lighter and easier to maintain. We were loading our guns when John finally came back to the subject.

"You can't divorce me, you know." He didn't look at me when he said it.

Oh, how I can kill that man right here and now!

Of course I knew I couldn't kill him. His parents had made me sign a prenuptial agreement in which it was stated that should the marriage fail or if John should die from unnatural causes proven to be caused by my hand, his estate wouldn't go to me. I now hated John with every fiber in my body, but the love for my lifestyle was greater. In my diary, I had written down available options, like untraceable poison, hiring a killer that couldn't be linked to me, and the likes. Anything to get me out of the chains that John had put me in.

I turned to him and said, "What are you going to do now?"

John slid the box of ammunition in his jacket pocket and closed the Remington with a snap.

"What do you think I can do?" His eyes looked up at me from under his bushy eyebrows.

The menacing tone of his voice made shivers run up and down my spine. All of a sudden, I didn't think it was such a good idea to go hunting today. My hands became sweaty and my heart was pounding in my chest. I was looking around to see if there were any witnesses around, but the only people here were the drivers of traffic passing by.

"Duck!" I yelled.

"Where?" said John as he looked up.

That was when the metal H-beam that came sliding off a truck that had jack-knifed for an unknown reason at that very moment and location smashed into Johns' head. He was dead before he hit the ground.

Problem solved.

Found Out!

Keywords: Surgeon, Cubicle, Homework, Beetroot

Brad was pulling his hairs out by now.

"I don't like these either," Mikey said. Mikey didn't like the fourth pair of pants that Brad had brought into the changing room. That was on top of the two pairs that they took with them to start with. Mikey threw the dark blue pants back at Brad, who stood just outside the dark curtain. The heat radiating off the multiple lights in the confined space was causing him to sweat. He wished he was outside, hitting a par three, instead of being on this shopping spree with Mikey that Madeline, his wife, had organized. She was the one that wanted Mikey to get new pants. She was the one that was supposed to have gone shopping with Mikey this afternoon. Why did her mother have to get sick today? Brad hated shopping, with a passion. He'd rather operate on a festered anal gland than go shopping. There had been no excuse not to take Mikey shopping though. He had taken the afternoon off to work on his speech for the BAAPS. The life of a plastic surgeon was never a dull one and as a highly regarded specialist in his field, he had to keep on top of things by writing numerous articles and giving speeches. Again, he'd rather reconstruct ten vaginas than going shopping with his son.

Don't get him wrong, he loved Mikey. Even though the lad was now six foot five, Madeline and Brad had kept calling him Mikey as he was growing into a fine young man. It was sort of their nickname for him now, letting him know he would always be their little boy. As Mikey kept on growing, so did his talent in sport. First, he had been picked to play on the basketball team. He had a great time there and was a good team player. As Mikey not only grew in height but also in width, the rugby team became very interested in him two years ago and, to the pain of the basketball coach, convinced Mikey to join their team. And he was good at it. His height and weight was a formidable sight and gave freight to all of his opponents. Brad was glad for the boy and he had even managed to see a couple of games.

"Okay, how about you go and have a look for what you *do* like, I've done all I could." Brad had had enough of this.

Mikey sighed.

"Fine, but you will have to stay with my stuff, I'm not leaving it unattended," Mikey said to his Dad.

"No worries, my feet are too sore to walk anymore anyway," Brad replied and took Mikey's place in the changing cubicle, whilst Mikey went in search of the mysterious likable pants.

Tired, Brad sat down on the little bench and looked at his image in the mirror. He was getting old. He didn't want reality to stare him in the face, so he looked for a distraction. Mikey's bag was huge. It contained all his rugby gear. Brad had picked Mikey up at the entrance of the mall, as Mikey's rugby friend had dropped him off just after training. Brad had offered to put it in the trunk of his car, but Mikey said he had no problem carrying it around. Brad glanced at the zipper of the large bag, which was slightly open.

After about ten minutes Mikey came back into the changing area. "Dad, I think I've found the perfect pair this time," he said enthusiastically as he threw open the curtain of the cubicle. "What the...?!" were his next word.

In the small cubicle stood his father, wearing his rugby kit over his underwear with his socks and shoes still on.

"What are you doing?!" Mikey said as he quickly stepped into the cubicle and shut the curtain clumsily behind him. His cheeks had gone bright red. Brad's face also had gone as red as a beetroot.

"I... I'm sorry, son," he stammered, "but I have always wanted to be a rugby player. I just wanted to find out what it was like to carry all that gear."

Mikey blinked. This was the most personal thing his father had ever said to him. Usually, it was more like 'go do your homework,' 'keep studying hard,' or words to that effect. Tears welled up in Mikey's eyes.

Brad looked at his son and felt the instant connection, the long-lost bond with his only son. He threw his arms around his son and they shared a big hug. Brad now was so happy he went shopping with Mikey.

Suddenly, the curtains were pushed aside by a male shop attendant.

"Only one person per cubicle!" he said sternly.

Brad and Mikey, still in their embrace, turned their heads and stared at the pimply redhead who was staring back at them with open mouth. Brad cleared his throat and let go of his son.

"Um, yes, of course. Don't worry about us. Just a father and son moment..."

Mikey stepped out of the cubicle as soon as he could, drawing the curtain shut again behind him.

"Are you taking those?" the attendant asked, pointing at the pants that Mikey was holding.

"Yes, yes I am," he said.

As soon as the attendant left he leaned against the wall and laughed out loud as he heard his father giggle.

Jake's Accomplice

<u>Writing Assignment</u>: A Western

The customers in the bank turned around.

"Stick 'em up!" Jake yelled.

Jake shot a bullet into the ceiling of the building. Instantly everybody stuck their hands up, knowing that Jake meant business. One woman fainted, and a few made little shrieks. Jake walked forward with a self-assured swagger and threw a hessian bag over the counter.

"Fill this one up in a hurry!" he said loudly to the teller. Before the man could reach below the counter, Jake pointed his Colt SSA at the man's face, leaned over and took the teller's Smith & Wesson out.

Jake was on top of the world. This was his third bank robbery. With the addition of this bank's loot, he could probably buy a little farm, get married and settle down. Pleased with himself, he looked around. The customers of the bank were eyeing him suspiciously. He saw one of them move his hands to his holster.

"I wouldn't do that if I were you," Jake warned him, "My gun may go off again... accidentally..."

The man retracted his hand slowly.

The teller was now slowly filling up the bag.

"For heaven's sake, man, hurry up! I haven't got all day!" And for good measure, he shot another bullet past the man's head. The teller, now fearing for his life, picked up the pace of placing the wads of money into the bag.

"You won't get out alive," one of the customers said.

Jake turned around.

"Who said that?"

"The bank has been expecting you, Jake. Your reputation precedes you," a man in a black suit said.

Jake took in the appearance of the man. He was lean, immaculately dressed, and neatly shaven. Jake saw that he was carrying as well.

"Is that so?" Jake chuckled. "Well, bless my soul, who would have thought that, eh?" he walked up to one of the customers. "Me, famous! Ha!" Jake seriously thought it was funny.

"The sheriff is already waiting for you outside," the man in black said. "As soon as you step out of this building with that money, you are a dead man," he continued.

Jake quickly glanced out of the windows, past their iron bars, and saw that somebody was leading the horses, which had been tied up in front of the bank, away, including his faithful appaloosa horse named Jengo.

"Lord Almighty, where are they taking my horse?" Jake exclaimed.

"See, you're can't get away now. It's better if you give me your pistol and surrender," the black-clad stranger said.

Jake's brain was going like a whirlwind now. He had to find a way out with the money, but without getting shot. Once outside his problems would be over.

"Alrighty, y'all stand in a line facing the wall, the lot of you," Jake said. He pushed them all to one side of the hall, including the lady that had fainted and had been brought to her wits again by one of the other ladies. He took all the pistols of the men out of their holsters and threw them to the other side of the room. He went over to the teller and took the bag with money from him. Jake took the arm of the lady that had been carrying the little pistol in the pouch attached to her wrist and turned her around.

"You're coming with me, sweetheart!" and he pushed her toward the doors. She gave a little shriek. Before he opened the doors, he said to the remaining customers and teller, "Now don't you lot try anything funny or the lovely lady gets it. And I mean it!" As a warning, he shot another bullet into the ceiling.

Jake opened the doors carefully. He didn't want to get the woman shot at first sight. Using her as a shield the both of them stepped out.

"Please, don't hurt me, Sir!" the woman wailed.

"Shut up or I'll have to shoot you in the head!" Jake replied.

As soon as his eyes had adjusted to the bright sunlight, he took in the opposition. There was the sheriff across the street, two men flanking him, one on the rooftop of the saloon and he was sure there was another one in the alley across the street away from the sheriff. He didn't see Jengo anywhere close by.

Jake put his thumb and index finger into his mouth and whistled loudly. At first, there was nothing, but all of a sudden, they heard galloping. Jengo came cantering around the corner, with a guy hanging on to the reins for dear life, being dragged through the dust by Jengo. He let go just after coming around the bend. Jengo stopped right in front of Jake.

"Get on the horse!" he yelled to the woman. The woman hurried to get on top of the stallion.

As Jake was readying himself to mount Jengo as well, the black-clad man came bursting through the bank doors, pistols drawn. Jake, who was now midway mounting his steed, wasn't in a position to do anything but look at the vision of death coming for him. All of a sudden there was a loud shot next to his ear and the black-clad man fell onto his back. A red patch stained the white shirt under the black three-piece suit. A deputy star was clearly visible on his chest now.

Jake looked up at the woman, who was holding out her hand for him. He grabbed it and hurriedly spurred Jengo on. Together they escaped under gunfire from the remaining law enforcers.

Not far from the little town they had just robbed, the woman and Jake stopped at a little cabin. Jake jumped off Jengo and stuck his hands out to help the woman off the horse.

"We did it!" he yelled and twirled her around before letting her touch the ground. He then kissed her tenderly. "Am I glad you thought of carrying that second gun, my love!"

"So did I, Jake. So did I!" she replied and kissed him again.

False Confession

Keywords: Orchard, Child, Fossil

She saw her sitting in the orchard under an apple tree. The child was sitting with her back against the medium-sized stem, both her arms wrapped around her knees and her face in a pout. As she walked closer, she saw that the child's brows were frowning. 'A five-year-old should not be this unhappy,' she thought to herself.

"Hey there," she called out to her, letting the child know her presence. "Why are you here? You should be having fun with the other children," she said and moved closer, hoping not to alarm the girl.

"I hate them," the girl said, her frown deepening even more.

"That's a bit harsh. Are you sure you know them that well?" the woman said as she sat down next to the girl. She plucked a stem of grass and twiddled with it in her hands.

"You're the actress, aren't you?" the girl said, cocking her head towards the tall, slender woman.

"Yes, I am," the woman said. "I am the actress. My name is Eva."

"Why should I talk to you? I don't know you. My Mom said never to talk to strangers," the girl said defiantly.

"That's very wise advice. Your Mom's obviously a very clever woman. But you know, sometimes it is good to talk to a stranger. Sometimes it is easier to talk to someone you don't know about your problems than to do so with somebody you do know." Eva looked at the little girl. "I hope you have realized by now that I'm not going to kidnap you or hurt you. Look at all the people on the veranda; they can all see us. You're safe." Eva looked away from the girl now, giving her the time to process the situation.

"They call me Ginny," the girl finally said.

"Nice to meet you, Ginny," Eva replied.

"My name is actually Georgia, but everybody calls me Ginny, because of my ginger hair." Ginny sighed heavily. Eva looked at the girl and understood what the problem was.

"You have beautiful red hair, I must say," she said with admiration and twirled a finger through one of Ginny's locks.

"I hate it!" Ginny said angrily as she pulled her head away and the lock out of Eva's hand. "They call me all sorts of names for it; carrot top, Fanta head, fire beacon, and, worst of all, ginger nut." Ginny put her chin on her knees again. A tear was rolling from her eye.

"I hope you know they're just jealous. Even I am jealous. Such beautiful red hair, I always wished I had red hair..." She made an extra heavy sigh whilst looking into the distance. She could feel Ginny's eyes on her.

"Beautiful red locks flowing in the wind, making my skin look extra pale and beautiful... I would be an even more famous actress if I had red hair." She smiled at Ginny.

"You think so?" Ginny asked, looking uncertain.

"I know so! My agent even asked me to dye my hair red one day," Eva said.

"Did you?" the girl asked wide-eyed.

"I tried, but my hair didn't want to take the dye. It is very hard to become a red-head, you know. Not everyone can do it. That's why it's so special."

Ginny put her chin on her knees again, but this time she seemed intrigued. Being aware that she had accomplished her task, Eva took her earrings out and gave them to Ginny.

"Here," she said, "why don't you show your friends these. They're made from real fossils which lived millions of years ago."

The girl was astounded and gasped at the earrings in her hand. "Thanks!" she said as she jumped up and ran to her friends. Eva smiled and after she saw the girl being the center of attention of her friends, she got up and walked back to the house.

"I see you have managed to cheer up Ginny," Eva's host, Michael, said. He handed Eva a glass of champagne and they both looked at the group of youngsters.

"Yes, I told her I always wanted to have red hair and that people who call red-head names are just jealous people," Eva explained.

Michael looked at Eva and frowned. "You really want to be a red-head?" he asked.

"Over my dead body," Eva whispered over her glass and took another sip before turning around and joining the others.

Love affairs

<u>Keywords</u>: Algebra, Rose, Restroom, Post Box

One, two, three... John counted in his head, even though he knew exactly how to waltz. Dancing was like algebra; it was pretty simple once you understood the formula. He liked the twist better, of course, but that new sound was the devil's music according to his parents.

All of a sudden, Lucy, his partner, made a wrong step and John noticed too late. He did quickly held back his foot, so he wouldn't step on her toes, but it made him lose balance and fall. Fortunately, he let go of Lucy, so he didn't take her with him.

"Oh dear!" Lucy said apologetically when John lay on the floor.

"It's ok. I'm ok," John said as he got up and dusted himself off.

"John, you really need to pay more attention," Mrs. Weathersby, the dance instructor, said sternly.

John cursed in his head. It hadn't been his fault, again. Why did Lucy pick him to dance with tonight? She was a nice enough girl, but she couldn't dance. Unlike Angela, who was an angel flying over the ballroom dancefloor. Angela was dancing with Peter at the moment. Everybody watched the perfect couple as they passed.

John had decided this morning to tell Angela how he felt about her. He had been in love with her since third grade but had never had the courage to talk to her. Maybe he could get her to notice him when they danced, but Peter was always in his way. 'Stupid Peter,' John thought. He had to admit, Peter was the male version of Angela. He was tall, handsome, and good at everything he did.

John wanted his moment with Angela to be perfect. 'First impressions are the most important,' his mother always said. He had bought a rose after school and had it in his jacket pocket. He had planned to walk up to her, offer the rose, and then to tell her how she compared to it.

When the music stopped, it was break time. Everybody flocked to the bar. 'It's now or never,' John thought. He looked around and spotted Angela. John pushed his way through the crowd to get to her. He pulled the rose out of his pocket. As he stepped past Dirk, he held the rose up and opened his mouth to talk. Angela turned her head and looked him in the eye. She had a beautiful smile. Then Peter moved between him and Angela and handed her a drink. Angela didn't look at him again. John put the rose back into his pocket. He went to the bar and got himself a drink. He waited patiently for the next perfect moment. Peter went to the restrooms. This was it! John wiped the sweat from his hands and turned around. He walked up to Angela and, again, held out the rose for her. This time she took the rose from him.

"Angela..." he started.

An awful pain exploded in his jaw and he was flying through the air. Peter had hit him.

"Peter! What are you doing?!" Angela screamed.

"Stay away from my girl," Peter said to John as he stood over him.

"I'm not your girl, Peter!" Angela yelled. John could see she was angry over Peter's statement. He tried to get up. Peter was about to whack him another one, but Angela held his arm, preventing Peter to strike again. John scrambled backward and wiped the blood off his lip. This was not going the way he wanted it to go at all. He got up and looked at Peter, then at Angela. They were arguing now. John turned around and fled to the men's restroom.

He looked into the mirror and saw his lip was swelling. He heard the door open and his best friend, Danny, came in.

"Are you okay?" Danny asked.

"I'll live," John answered.

"Here, let me have a look at that," Danny said as he wetted a paper towel. He let Danny wipe the new blood from his lip. It was getting painful now.

"Ouch! Be careful!" he said as he pushed Danny's hand away.

"I know something for the pain," Danny said. His eyes were gentle, and he took John's face in his hands. He moved his face closer and pouted his lips. John realized that Danny was about to kiss him. With all his might he pulled his head back.

"I'm ok. It's ok. It doesn't hurt anymore," he said. He pulled Danny's hands off his face and fled from the restroom. What was Danny thinking? John tried to compose himself. Could it be that his best friend was... gay? No way! He would have known, wouldn't he? John was confused now. First being hit by Peter, then hit on by Danny. Why were all of the people around him acting like aliens? Could it get any worse? He went back to the dancefloor and danced the second half of the lesson with Lucy. Peter kept looking at him over his shoulder and whenever he did John quickly looked away. Whenever he saw Angela, John noticed that she wasn't happy and that there definitely was a distance between her and Peter.

After the lesson ended, John waited until the crowd had left before leaving himself. He couldn't face Angela tonight after fleeing from Peter. He certainly didn't want to face Danny again tonight. Tomorrow, he was going to pretend nothing had happened on that front. When the others were gone, he zipped up his jacket and went outside. His eye caught movement to the left. He saw Angela standing in the shadows. Could it be she had been waiting for him? He turned towards her, but then saw she was kissing. He took another look. He wasn't mistaken, Angela was kissing another girl! John couldn't believe his eyes. What was it with people tonight? He walked off into the night. He came to a post box and banged his head against it. Maybe the memories of this night would leave him this way. He noticed someone step from behind the post box. Still leaning against the red pillar, he turned his head and saw it was Lucy. She walked up to him with a smile on her face. With her delicate, gloved hands, she lifted his head off the post box and held his face close to hers.

"I know I'm not a good dancer, and I don't look like Angela," she said. "I may not even be human, but I do love you." Her eyes glowed a neon-green before she kissed him.

John felt her hot lips on his and thought 'If you can't beat them, join them,' and happily kissed her back.

Santa

<u>Writing Assignment</u>: A Christmas story
<u>Keywords</u>: New York, a family with kids, 1940-ish.

New York, 1940, Macy's Department Store

The boy shuffled to the perfume display. His hair standing up in all directions, his coat too small and worn, his nose and hands red from the cold outside.

"Get away, boy! Scram!" Mr. Stuart, the new floor manager, yelled.

"No, no, it's okay. Leave him," Linsey said. She put her hand on Mr. Stuart's shoulder. He looked at it, annoyed, before looking her in the eye. Linsey took her hand off as fast as she could, holding it with her other hand as if to prevent it from doing something stupid again. As a mere counter attendant, it was not done to touch your superior, let alone tell him what to do.

"It's okay, Mr. Stuart. Sam is okay," she dared again. Before he could tell her otherwise, Linsey walked up to the counter to help the boy, who shyly smiled at her. He pointed at one of the perfume bottles, a Chanel No.5 one. Linsey's smile grew as she took the bottle from the counter display and sprayed a little of the expensive perfume into the air. Sam waved his bared wrist through the expensive vapor and then smelled his wrist. A large smile appeared on his face. At the same time, tears filled his eyes.

"That's enough now," Mr. Stuart said to the boy. He had been watching the spectacle intently. "Get out before I call security."

Sam looked up at the stern face of Mr. Stuart. As he turned away, a tear rolled over his cheek. Linsey and Mr. Stuart stood behind the counter watching the boy leave, who was smelling his wrist again and again.

"What was that all about?" Mr. Stuart asked. "We can't have this sort of scum in here. They'll scare away the customers."

"Oh, but Sam is not scum, Mr. Stuart," Linsey replied.

"Well, he certainly looks like scum according to my dictionary."

"Sam and his mother used to come here often to buy perfume. Chanel No.5 was her favorite. That's why he always comes in here to get a sample."

"Would his mother be able to afford such an expensive brand?"

"Oh yes! The Matthews were very rich people. They came to buy here at Macy's all the time. But that's no more..."

"Why? What happened?" asked Mr. Stuart.

"It's a very sad story. Two years ago, Mrs. Matthews became very ill. Apparently, she got a horrible disease. No matter what doctors did, they couldn't help her. She died two years ago. Mr. Matthews was heartbroken and became depressed. He no longer cared for anything and began drinking. He lost his job at the stock market. He lost everything. Sam and his sister, Hannah, sometimes come here and ask for a sample of Chanel No.5. They never buy anything anymore. What they really come in for is to relive the memory of their mother." Linsey wiped away a tear that had appeared in the corner of her eye. The thought of the children trying to hold on to the memory of their deceased mother pained her every time she thought of it. "Oh well, nothing to be done about it," she said as she made herself busy rearranging the display again.

Mr. Stuart looked at Linsey and then at the exit the boy had just used to leave the department store.

The next week, Sam and Hannah came in wearing new coats, ones that fit them perfectly. They both had huge smiles on their faces.

"My, what happened to you lovely people?" Linsey asked as the two children stood eagerly in front of the perfume counter. Her new floor manager, Mr. Brown, came to inspect the children as well.

"Daddy got a job!" Hannah said. She twirled around in her new coat. "And we got new coats!"

"I can see that," Linsey said. "You look fabulous in it!" She turned to Sam.

"Yes, a guy came up to Dad in the street the other day and offered him a job in the finance department of this warehouse. Can you believe it?"

"No!" Linsey exclaimed. That was the most unlikely story she had heard of in a long time. "Just like that?"

"Yes, just like that. Isn't it great?" Sam's smile was so big, it nearly split his face in two.

In the meantime, Linsey had already taken out the Chanel No.5 perfume bottle. Both kids held out their wrists and she sprayed them both. The wonderful smell wafted through the air as the kids waved their arms about. The focus of the children's eyes went into space, into a time gone by, when they smelled their wrists.

"Thank you," Sam said.

"Anytime," Linsey replied.

Sam nodded, and he and his sister turned around. Together they left the store, hugging each other.

The rest of the day, sales were lower than expected so close to Christmas. Not too many customers could afford expensive gifts like perfume anymore. The war in Europe didn't make people spend that much on luxuries over here.

"Come on, Linsey. We've got to go to the meeting," Mr. Brown said at the end of the day.

"Ah yes, the meeting." Linsey didn't want to go to the boring end-of-year meeting. It was just a lot of blah-blah about how times were tough and how much harder they had to work to sell more, but everyone had been told to go. They closed the till and took the elevator to the warehouse part of the building. It was the only space large enough for all staff to be in at once.

Linsey wasn't a tall girl and standing at the back of the crowd didn't help her gain interest in what was said. She was picking at her nails when she suddenly heard a voice she recognized. She looked up but couldn't see.

"Who's talking?" she asked Mr. Brown.

"It's Mr. Klein, the new store manager," Mr. Brown said.

Linsey didn't know Mr. Klein as he had just been appointed. She had to know for sure though, so she worked her way to the front of the crowd.

There, in a Santa suit, stood a small man. He was telling staff how well they had worked and how proud he was of them. Then, as his speech nearly ended, he took off his Santa hat and Linsey recognized him as Mr. Stuart, her temporary floor manager.

As Linsey stood there looking at the miracle that was her new boss. A little twinkle gleamed in Mr. Klein's eyes as their eyes met. He then continued to address the other staff.

'He truly is Santa,' Linsey thought and couldn't stop smiling.

Vampires Anonymous

<u>Last but not least</u>: This is one of the stories I wrote for the Twisted50 competition but didn't make the cut

A man in black stood in front of a seated, dark-dressed crowd.

"Hi, my name is George. I'm a vampire and I didn't drink any human blood for forty-seven days now."

"Well done, George! Please give George an applause, everyone!" said Steve, the group's social worker. He stood up enthusiastically and did most of the applauding. The vampires in his group were getting rather listless lately, and he wasn't sure what to do about it. Steve had started 'Vampires Anonymous' in his neighborhood as the issue had been getting out of hand. Every morning, he had to step over several drained bodies on his way to work at the church and people were complaining about the stench. The police did their best trying to work out which vampire had not been keeping to their quota of two victims a week. Getting evidence for this took time as the vampires didn't leave their business cards. As a result, bodies kept lying around and the situation was becoming a health hazard.

Steve had acquired experience in helping people with problems whilst running his 'Alcoholics Anonymous' group and thought he'd give it a go to help the vampires.

The turnout wasn't great at first, but as soon as he changed the meeting's location from the church to the school, numbers had been steadily rising. Steve thought his enthusiastic teachings were the magnet, although he did realize the fact that caught quota-trespassers were lawfully required to seek treatment may have something to do with it as well.

"Well done. Please sit down again, George. Who's next?" Steve asked the group. "You there, in the black, no, the other one, please come forward."

A pale man stood up and shuffled toward the stage. His skin was as white as marble and his features gaunt. Once in front of the others, he turned and sighed.

"Hello everyone, my name is Adam. I'm a vampire and I have not drained a human from blood for one whole day." He hung his head as he said it.

Instantly there was a shock-wave going through the attendees.

"Adam," Steve said, "I am so disappointed to hear this. You were going so well! You nearly beat Jenny's record last week."

Jenny was now beaming in her chair, knowing she was still record holder.

"I'm sorry, but you know the rules, Adam," Steve continued. It was now Steve's turn to sigh. He turned toward the crowd and said, "Okay, guys, give him your best shot." Steve really didn't like this part of the meetings.

Everybody got up, filed into the middle aisle, picked up an overripe tomato from the greengrocer's box and, one by one, they threw it at Adam. Red juice dripped from his eyebrow and nose, seeds sticking to his skin like pimples. It was not a pretty sight. Everybody, except for Adam, sat down again. If Steve didn't like this part of the meeting, the vampires were as happy as cattle brought to the slaughter about it. They slumped back in their seats and sought obscurity amongst their black attire trying not to be picked out by Steve as the next victim.

"How did that feel, Adam? Did that feel good?" Steve asked the vampire. The man silently shook his head, tomato seeds flying off his nose. "No, it doesn't, does it. Remember this feeling next time you think of sinking your teeth into a juicy neck.

At these words, a murmur went through the crowd and more than half of the attendees sat upright in their seats.

'Oops, wrong choice of words,' thought Steve, 'let's quickly move on.'

"Okay, who's next?" His gaze went around the room.

Tina stood up eagerly and came forward. She was a lovely looking Goth with black lipstick and all. She dragged a young man by his sleeve behind her.

Steve rejoiced as it was the first time someone volunteered. 'My enthusiasm is finally rubbing off,' he thought and smiled.

"Hi, my name is Tina, and I am a vampire." Tina had a typical Southern American accent. "I have not drunk human blood for twenty-eight days now and I brought my nephew, Vlad."

"Well done, Tina! Applause for Tina everybody!" Steve said while applauding so hard his hands began to tingle.

Only two or three vampires clapped with him. Steve looked at the young man standing next to Tina.

"So, Vlad, nice to have you here. Please tell us a bit more about yourself."

Vlad looked uncomfortable at his aunt, but she prodded him to speak.

"Hi, everybody. My name is Vlad and I am from Transylvania vere ve do not have groups like dese."

"Oh, interesting," said Steve. "How does your country deal with the drinking problem?" Steve thought it was a clever question and was sure the answer would show how far advanced the USA was compared to Eastern European countries.

"Ve don't see it as a problem," Vlad answered. He immediately had everybody's attention.

"Please explain," Adam said, fascinated, still wiping the tomato juice off his face.

"Ve used to be a poor country, our tourism industry suffering badly from so many tourists disappearing. But den ve changed de laws and now ve drink beggars, alcoholics, and addicts only. Our lives have improved.

Once ve had no more people boddering de tourists, dey returned, bringing deir money wiz dem."

"But that's discrimination!" Steve said slightly louder than he had wanted to.

"He's got a point though," George said.

"Two," giggled Tina, and pointed at her fangs.

"We also have so much unwanted folk in *our* country. We could do with a bit of a clean-up like that," Adam added.

"That's preposterous," Steve cried, getting rather red in the face now. The goal of the group treatment was to stop the vampires killing people altogether and, at the moment, that idealism was disappearing like blood from a vampire's victim. "Tourists are still disappearing from your country," he tried to throw in as a counterbalance.

"Vell, you can't deny de tourists from your country do look plump and juicy!" Vlad laughed. All the group attendees laughed with him. "I mean, look at yourself, you look like you're a nice fast-food meal if I may say so!"

All eyes turned to Steve. The vampires began to lick their lips.

"Hang on, no... guys wait, I'm not plump. It's my jumper, it makes me look poofy."

The vampires, however, were hungry, very hungry. Steve could see it in their eyes. He finally realized why they had been so listless lately. The vampires got out of their seats and corralled Steve like they were herding their next ~~stake~~ steak.

"Okay, time out now. Have a coffin break!" Steve said. "Did I tell you about the planned water-skiing trip on Lake Eerie?" He desperately tried to avert the vampires' attention.

Unfortunately, it didn't work. As one they fell on Steve and had him for dinner.

Afterward, Adam shook Vlad's hand and thanked him.

Vlad smiled. "The name's James, actually. James Jenkins. I'm a hired actor from LA." He then turned to Tina. "And you owe me a few dollars."

Tina wiped a streak of blood from the corner of her mouth and smiled.

If you liked my short stories, why not read my novels?

RELEASING A VAMPIRE

Prequel

Settle into a cozy corner with this novelette and find out about the events that lead up to the action-packed, suspenseful urban fantasy yet funny Suckers Trilogy.

Who created the deadly *Succedaneum* virus? What was it meant to do? How did it escape into the world?

What relationship did Kate have with Charlie before the virus broke out? What was her life like when Black October began? How did Kate deal with her world falling apart?

LIVING LIKE A VAMPIRE

Book 1

Kate is trying very hard to stay alive in a world thrown into chaos. Charlie is trying very hard to get Kate to notice him. When Caleb comes to the scene, things change, but is it for the better?

Kate had just begun her new job as a high school science teacher and was looking forward to living a suburban dream life. All her hopes and dreams turn into smoke as a virus turns people into vampires roaming the world in packs and killing everybody they can get their hands on. Together with her friends Sue and Charlie, she hides at a campground. They think they are safe there. They are wrong.

They are attacked by a pack of suckers and Kate has to flee again. She gets separated from her friends, accidentally bumps into a handsome sucker who then mysteriously disappears, after which she has to pretend to be a sucker to stay alive. Having met Caleb, surviving is no longer the only thing on Kate's mind.

RAISING A VAMPIRE
Book 2

Kate and her little family have led a quiet life. An unfortunate event sees Kate following her daughter into prison. Events drive the happy family apart.

One day, Kate makes the mistake to invite a colleague into her home. He betrays her trust and commits an act of violence. When Kate's daughter comes to the rescue, she exposes herself for what she really is; a sucker. Kate accompanies her daughter when she is sent to a sucker internment camp. The situation quickly spirals downhill when an old flame from the past turns up and rekindles Kate's love for him.

Once more, Kate is thrown into turmoil and heartache.

Join Kate as she struggles with the amorous feelings that awaken after meeting her old flame. Feel her pain as she loses the friendship of a good friend, as she pushes her daughter away from her instead of keeping her on the right path, and as she tries to stay faithful to her partner.

Can Kate keep her family and her wits together?

KILLING A VAMPIRE
Book 3

The past is back to haunt Kate. Will her partner survive this evil?

Kate thinks her relationship is on the rocks because of her past infidelity. She's wrought with guilt and wants nothing more than her missing partner back. When the police don't believe there's foul play at hand she's on her own to find him. A horrifying parcel arriving on Kate's doorstep brings the situation to a whole new lever. The police are now willing but can't due to lack of evidence.

There is one person able to help Kate, but everybody warns her not to accept his helping hand. How far is Kate willing to go to save the one she loves?

Killing a Vampire explores the emotional bonds between mother and child, sisters, and lovers. Follow the hints and clues as Kate explores the depth of her emotions while trying to save her love.

About the Author

Jacky Dahlhaus has worked many jobs and tried many hobbies before she realized writing gave her such pleasure. She loves to write paranormal fantasy stories while delving into the human psyche with all its faults and mysteries.

Next to writing novels, Jacky helps indie authors by promoting them on her blog, writes an online newsletter/magazine, runs a writing club for adults and for children at the local library, and is a director for Aberdeenshire Film Productions.

When not busy with the above (which is rare nowadays), Jacky works on renovating her Scottish Victorian home, watches movies with her family, and tries to stop her two Jack Russells from barking for no good reason.

Jacky continues writing short stories and will publish them on a regular basis.

jackydahlhaus.com

Connect

I'd love to hear from you personally too!
You can connect with me via:

Email:
jackydahlhaus@gmail.com

Twitter:
https://twitter.com/JackyDahlhaus

Instagram:
https://www.instagram.com/jackydahlhaus/

Facebook:
https://www.facebook.com/Jacky-Dahlhaus-Author-166614624053352/

My Website:
https://jackydahlhaus.com

Thank you so much for reading, and I hope to read your review soon, see your name on my mailing list, and be able to send you my next book!

Jacky Dahlhaus